Miss Smith Reads Again!

MICHAEL GARLAND

▪ DUTTON CHILDREN'S BOOKS ▪

To Peggy III

DUTTON CHILDREN'S BOOKS
A division of Penguin Young Readers Group

Published by the Penguin Group
Penguin Group (USA) Inc., 375 Hudson Street, New York, New York 10014, U.S.A. • Penguin Group (Canada), 90 Eglinton
Avenue East, Suite 700, Toronto, Ontario, Canada M4P 2Y3 (a division of Pearson Penguin Canada Inc.) • Penguin Books
Ltd, 80 Strand, London WC2R 0RL, England • Penguin Ireland, 25 St Stephen's Green, Dublin 2, Ireland (a division of
Penguin Books Ltd) • Penguin Group (Australia), 250 Camberwell Road, Camberwell, Victoria 3124, Australia (a division
of Pearson Australia Group Pty Ltd) • Penguin Books India Pvt Ltd, 11 Community Centre, Panchsheel Park, New Delhi—
110 017, India • Penguin Group (NZ), Cnr Airborne and Rosedale Roads, Albany, Auckland 1310, New Zealand (a division
of Pearson New Zealand Ltd) • Penguin Books (South Africa) (Pty) Ltd, 24 Sturdee Avenue, Rosebank, Johannesburg 2196,
South Africa • Penguin Books Ltd, Registered Offices: 80 Strand, London WC2R 0RL, England

CIP Data is available

Published in the United States by Dutton Children's Books,
a division of Penguin Young Readers Group
345 Hudson Street, New York, New York 10014
www.penguin.com/youngreaders

Manufactured in China • First Edition
0-525-47722-5
1 3 5 7 9 10 8 6 4 2

School used to be humdrum and boring. Not anymore! Now that Miss Smith was his teacher, Zack looked forward to going every day.

Each new day meant Miss Smith would read a different tale from her *Incredible Storybook*. This book was like no other. When she read from it, the classroom would change and the story would come alive. And when it was over, everything would *whoosh* back into the book.

Miss Smith would always remind the class when she began to read: "Remember, class, don't interfere with the characters, or you'll change the story and it won't end the way it should! The story has to end—otherwise it won't go back into the book."

One day Miss Smith said, "Today we have a very special story, Arthur Conan Doyle's *The Lost World*."

Zack was so excited, because *this* story was about dinosaurs. Zack loved dinosaurs!

As soon as Miss Smith started to read, the classroom began to change into the deepest, steamiest, most remote jungle of the Amazon.

Then the class found themselves on a fallen tree that bridged the gap between the outside world and the steep cliffs of the plateau that was called the Lost World.

"Don't look down!" Zack warned as one by one they crossed over.

When they reached the other side, they could feel the air was different. They heard strange bellowing sounds echoing through the trees. And they saw some men, off in the distance, threading their way through the prehistoric rainforest. Two of them wore khaki suits and helmets and carried backpacks.

"Who are they?" asked Sue Ann.

"They're dinosaur-hunting explorers," answered Miss Smith. "Remember, don't bother them, because you'll change the story and it may not end the way it should."

They followed along until they came close enough to hear the two explorers arguing. Miss Smith and the class hid in the bushes and listened.

"Professor Challenger, it is impossible for dinosaurs to still exist. There is simply no evidence!" said the tall explorer.

"Professor Summerlee, I beg to disagree!" answered the short one.

As Challenger and Summerlee continued their heated debate, a huge *Tyrannosaurus rex* stole up behind them.

Zack's eyes stared at the jagged fangs of the *T. rex,* but before Miss Smith could stop him, Zack screamed, "Look out behind you!!"

oth explorers turned. Then Professor Challenger snatched Summerlee away—just before the *Tyrannosaurus rex* pounced on the pair of them.

Run!" yelled Miss Smith as the class scattered in every direction.

"Do you need any more evidence, Professor Summerlee?" asked Zack as they looked for a place to hide.

Zack knew that *Tyrannosaurus* was very nearsighted. So they ducked into some bushes, and the king of the dinosaurs raced off without eating anyone.

Luckily, the professors, Zack, and the rest of the class managed to escape the *T. rex* and find one another, but Miss Smith was nowhere to be seen.

"Where is Miss Smith?" asked Sue Ann. "I don't see her anywhere!"

Just then, another dinosaur came into view. Some of the kids got ready to run away again, but Zack told them, "Don't worry. That's a *Stegosaurus*. They're herbivores. Stegosaurs eat only vegetation, so they're harmless— just like big cows."

We need to find Miss Smith right now. Maybe she's in danger. Don't forget, she has to finish reading the story!" Zack told the class.

"Look!" said Sue Ann. "Footprints! Let's follow them!"

It was easy for the class to follow Miss Smith's trail, because her sneakers left very distinctive footprints in the mud. They followed the tracks for a short distance, until suddenly they disappeared.

"Help! Help!" came a faint voice from high above them.

It was Miss Smith. She was trapped in a pterodactyl's nest on a tree branch hanging way out over a steep ravine. The flying dinosaur must have snatched her up and put her in the nest.

We have to save her!" everyone cried.

"I have a plan," said Zack. He quickly told the class what to do.
They broke off branches, and some of them climbed the tree.
When they reached the nest, they thrashed their
leafy weapons around until they scared the
pterodactyl away. Miss Smith collected
herself and carefully climbed out of
the nest and down the tree.

Thank you, class. You saved me!" Miss Smith said. "Now I think it's time we finish reading this story and go back to our classroom."

She started reading, and by the time she got to the last line, the dinosaurs, the explorers, and the lost world had gone back into the book, and their classroom had returned to normal.

Everything from the story had returned into the book—except for one thing. Somehow Zack was able to hold onto the pterodactyl egg.

The class crowded around the egg for a closer look. Then they heard it—a tiny scratching sound, then a louder tapping, and then an even louder cracking, then "SCREEEEEEEEECH!"

The little flying reptile burst from its shell and flapped around the room over their heads. Before they could close their open mouths, the baby pterodactyl flew out the window and off into the sky.

As Zack watched the winged creature soar off into the clouds, he couldn't help think of all the wonderful places reading Miss Smith's *Incredible Storybook* had taken them.

"Hmm, I wonder what tomorrow's story will be?"